MYTHOPEDIA

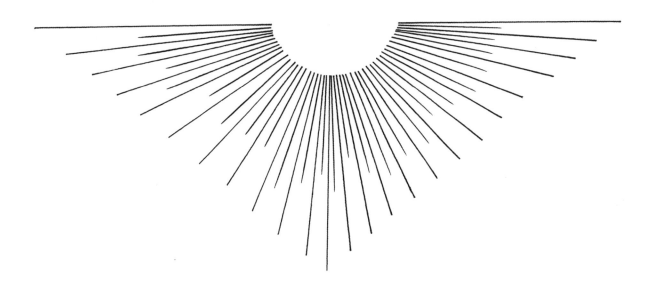

First published in Great Britain in 2020 by
Laurence King Publishing

5 7 9 10 8 6

Text © Anna Claybourne 2020
Illustrations © Good Wives and Warriors 2020

Good Wives and Warriors have asserted their right
under the copyright, designs and patents act 1988, to be identified as the author of this work.

A CIP catalogue record for this book
is available from the British Library.

ISBN 978-1-78627-691-9

Printed and bound in China

Laurence King Publishing
An imprint of
Hachette Children's Group
Part of Hodder and Stoughton
Carmelite House
50 Victoria Embankment
London EC4Y 0DZ

An Hachette UK Company
www.hachette.co.uk
www.hachettechildrens.co.uk

www.laurenceking.com

Laurence King Publishing is committed to ethical
and sustainable production. We are proud participants in the Book Chain Project®
Bookchainproject.com

GOOD WIVES AND WARRIORS

MYTHOPEDIA

AN ENCYCLOPEDIA OF
MYTHICAL BEASTS
AND THEIR MAGICAL TALES

CONTENTS

THE MYTHICAL WORLD

Myths and legends are ancient, traditional tales that have been passed from one person to another, often for generations. These stories tell of mysterious and magical creatures that live among us. Some of these beings could be mistaken for familiar animals, such as hares, horses, and squirrels, but can give themselves away by speaking, changing shape, casting spells, or suddenly growing to an enormous size. Others are outwardly fantastical and more easily spotted, such as dragons and unicorns, the Basilisk with its deadly venom, or the giant, water-loving Rainbow Serpent.

Why are these stories told? Some warn us about terrifying beasts, like the half-snake, half-elephant Grootslang, while others are simply to entertain—take, for instance, the tale of the shapeshifting Tanuki, who turns into a tea kettle. Often these rich tales help to explain how things came to be as they are: how the Thunderbird created storms, or how Anansi the spider god gave stories to humans.

The world of mythological beasts, therefore, is one filled with mystery and magic. With this encyclopedia as our guide, we will travel around the world discovering these wonderful creatures and their fascinating stories.

OUR

MYTHICAL WORLD

THE

AMERICAS

NORTH
ATLANTIC
OCEAN

PACIFIC
OCEAN

SOUTH
ATLANTIC
OCEAN

THE AMERICAS

Sweeping from the icy Arctic north, past the Equator,
to the mountains of Patagonia, this region boasts the mythical
monsters of the Amazon jungle, powerful Native American spirit
animals, and fabulous stories about how the world began.

QUETZALCOATL

The feathered serpent, god of light and the wind,
who created the humans of today

Long, long ago, say the Aztec legends, the first god, Ometeotl, created itself out of nothingness. Ometeotl was both good and evil, light and dark, mother and father. It had four children, all gods themselves, and the kindest, most humble of those gods is Quetzalcoatl, the feathered serpent.

Quetzalcoatl is the god of light, the dawn, the winds, and the West, and the guardian of art, science, books, and learning. Each morning he leads the Sun out of the underworld, where it goes at night, so that it can rise again.

Quetzalcoatl discovered corn, and showed it to humans so that they could grow food. He also gave them the calendar. He always cares for humans and protects them from danger. That's because it was he who created them, after all the previous worlds, and all the people in them, were destroyed…

How QUETZALCOATL CREATED HUMANS

In the beginning, the first god, Ometeotl, had four children. They were Quetzalcoatl, god of light; Tezcatlipoca, god of darkness; Huitzilopochtli, god of war; and Xipe Totec, god of farming and spring.

These gods created other gods, and a giant crocodile, Cipactli. But Cipactli swallowed everything else they created. So they divided her body into pieces. Her head became the heavens, her body became the Earth, and her tail became the underworld. Then the gods created the first people, a race of giants. But Tezcatlipoca fought with Quetzalcoatl, and, in a rage, sent his jaguars to eat all the giants.

The gods tried again, creating smaller humans this time. But, after another argument, Tezcatlipoca turned all the humans into monkeys.

The third time they tried, Tezcatlipoca ran away with Xochiquetzal, the wife of Tlaloc, god of rain. Tlaloc was so upset, he made it rain fire, burning the people and the Earth to ashes.

The fourth time, Tezcatlipoca teased the water goddess Chalchiuhtlicue, and she cried tears of blood, drowning the world in a red flood.

The fifth time, the god Quetzalcoatl decided to bring all the humans from the previous ages back to life. He asked Xolotl, the dog-headed god of the sunset, to take him to the underworld. When they arrived, they found the Lord and Lady of the Dead sitting on their thrones, attended by spiders, bats, and owls. Around them lay the bones of all the humans who had died in the four ages gone by.

"My Lord and Lady," Quetzalcoatl began. "I have come to take these bones, so that I can bring the humans back to life."

"No!" said the Lady of the Dead. "Why should we give you our precious bones? We will never get them back, and they belong to us. Go away."

"Don't worry, my Lady," said Quetzalcoatl. "I will not steal the bones, only borrow them. Eventually, each human will die, and their bones will come back to you."

"Very well," said the Lord of the Dead. "You may have the bones, as long as you can do one thing. Take this conch shell, and play beautiful music on it." He handed them a normal conch shell, which could not play music, and smiled smugly, because he was sure the task was impossible.

Quetzalcoatl called on the worms and the bees to help him. The worms nibbled holes in the shell, so that it could play different notes. The bees flew inside and buzzed, and beautiful music came out. The Lord and Lady of the Dead were furious, but they handed over the bones, and Quetzalcoatl and Xolotl set off.

However, the Lord and Lady had ordered their servants to dig pits around the underworld, to stop Quetzalcoatl from leaving. He fell into one of the pits, and all the bones broke. But he scooped up the pieces, and Xolotl helped him out of the pit, and at last they escaped.

Then Quetzalcoatl took the bones to Cihuacóatl, the snake goddess. She ground them up and mixed them with drops of Quetzalcoatl's blood, and they became humans. They lived in the fifth world, the one that still exists today. When Quetzalcoatl had taught them his wisdom, he transformed into the morning star and went to live in the sky.

MAPINGUARI

One-eyed, two-mouthed terror of the rainforest

According to local legends, a reddish, bear-like beast
roams through the undergrowth of the Amazon
rainforest: the monstrous Mapinguari. Though it's very
big, it is skilled at sneaking slowly and silently through
the jungle, so if a Mapinguari is nearby, you won't always
hear it. However, you might smell it, as its matted fur
gives off a revolting stench of garlic, dung, and rotting meat.

Once you do spot it, the Mapinguari is a terrifying sight.
It has one huge eye in the middle of its forehead, powerful
jaws, and long, backward-facing claws on its feet. When it
spots a human, it rears up on its hind legs, towering more than
six feet tall and revealing a second, gaping mouth with
razor-sharp teeth in the middle of its belly!

It's also known as the roaring beast, on account of its
bloodcurdling, screaming growl. Under its fur, its skin is
armored like a crocodile's, and no bullets or arrows can harm it.
Some say the Mapinguari is a vegetarian, but there are other
reports of it rampaging through farms, eating cows. It rarely attacks
people, but can easily destroy anyone who gets in its way.

The Mapinguari does have one weakness, however:
it hates water. And the rainforest has countless
rivers, streams, and pools, which can stop it
in its tracks. As long as there's a stream between
you and the beast, you're safe!

MICHABO

Magical great hare who rebuilt the world

The Algonquin people tell many tales about Michabo,
the Great Hare. Michabo is the giver of life, the creator
of humans, and Lord of deer and fish. He is the spirit
of the rising Sun, and ruler of the winds, the weather,
and the air. He is the god of invention, and
knows everything there is to know.

No one is sure where Michabo lives. Some say his home is
an island in the Great Lakes, and some say it's an iceberg in the
northern ocean. According to others, Michabo lives in the sky,
or far away in the east, where the Sun rises. Michabo's father
is the West Wind, and his mother is the Dawn, daughter
of the Moon, who is Michabo's grandmother.

Many years ago Michabo created the world as we know
it today, after it was destroyed by a great flood…

19

MICHABO
AND THE FLOOD

The story goes that one day Michabo the Great Hare, Lord of all the animals, was out hunting with his pack of trained wolves. As the wolves bounded ahead, they all ran together into a lake, and disappeared beneath the water. Michabo was puzzled, because this had never happened before. He followed the wolves into the lake to look for them, but the water rose up around him, higher and higher, and became a mighty, rushing flood that drowned the whole world.

When the water calmed, there was no land in sight at all. Michabo wanted to recreate the world, but even his magic could not rebuild a whole world from nothing. He needed a little piece of earth or soil to start off with, and he called on the other animals to help him.

Flying high in the sky above was the raven. "Raven!" Michabo cried. "Fly across the water and look for land, then bring me back some soil so that I can rebuild the world." The raven flew for many miles, searching for land as far as his sharp eyes could see. But he saw only water, and returned to Michabo with nothing.

Next Michabo asked the otter. "Otter," he ordered, "swim fast and far through the ocean, and find me some land. Bring me back a piece of it, to build a new world with." The otter swam away at once. But no matter how far he swam, his feet never found land. When he returned many hours later, he too had nothing.

Just then, the muskrat swam up to Michabo. "I can help," she said. And she dived down, deep below the waves, to the bottom of the flood, where the mud of the old Earth remained. She scooped some of it up in her claws and swam back to the surface, where Michabo was waiting.

Taking the mud in his paws, Michabo used his magic to turn it into an island, which he then set in place in the ocean. It grew and grew, becoming a great land, with mountains and valleys, rivers, meadows, grass, and trees. But the trees were nothing but bare, dry trunks, with no branches.

Michabo fitted an arrow to his magic bow, and fired it into the trunk of a tree. It immediately became a branch, and sprouted fresh green leaves. Michabo fired more and more arrows, covering every tree with branches laden with leaves, flowers, and fruit. The new world was more beautiful, lush, and green than the old one had ever been.

Then Michabo turned to the muskrat, and asked her to marry him. They lived happily together, and their children were the first humans. They became the mother and father of the whole human race, who spread out to live all over the new world Michabo had created.

From that day on, Michabo has always helped his children, the humans. He gave them picture writing, and woven nets for fishing. He visits them in their dreams, and whispers to them about the best places to go hunting and fishing. And each day he brings sunlight, so that the humans can find their way, build their homes, hunt, gather food, and live in happiness.

AHUIZOTL

Deadly water-dog with a taste for eyeballs

In Aztec folklore, the Ahuizotl lurks in the lakes and ponds around the great city of Tenochtitlan. This dangerous beast resembles a cross between a dog and an otter, with sleek black fur that stands up in spikes (its name means "spiky water creature"). It has sharp teeth, grasping paws, and, at the end of its long black tail, a human-like hand. This is what it uses to catch its prey—unwary fishermen.

The Ahuizotl is a guardian of the water, and protects the fish that live there. So, when a fisherman approaches, the creature swims up to him beneath the surface, then reaches out with its terrifying tail and grabs him by the ankle. It pulls him underwater to drown, then feasts on its favorite parts: the unlucky victim's eyeballs, teeth, and fingernails.

Sometimes, the Ahuizotl catches other victims, too, so anyone standing too close to the water's edge is at risk. And if it's especially hungry, the cunning creature hides and makes a wailing sound, just like the cries of a baby. When people come to the river to look for the child, the Ahuizotl grabs them.

There's only one silver lining to this watery fate. Because victims of the Ahuizotl die by drowning, their souls go to live with Tlaloc, god of rain and water, in the warm, sunlit paradise of Tlalocan, where it is always springtime.

THUNDERBIRD

The giant bird whose wingbeats make the thunder

According to northwest American native folklore, the Thunderbird is the greatest of all spirit animals. As he flies, his wings create the sound of thunder. His eyes burn with fire, and lightning bolts flash out of them. He is so huge and strong that he can pluck a whale out of the sea and carry it through the sky, as an eagle carries a fish.

Some say the Thunderbird lives on a faraway floating mountain, on the other side of the ocean. Others say he lives in a cloud. He stores his whale meat under the glaciers of the Olympic Mountains, in a deep ice cave.

The Thunderbird causes great thunderstorms, deadly lightning, and whirling winds. But the storms also bring rain, which waters the land and helps the crops to grow. And when humans are in trouble, the Thunderbird may come to the rescue…

THUNDERBIRD
AND THE WHALE

T his story comes from the Quileute people, who live in the
northwestern United States, near the Pacific Ocean.
Thousands of years ago, they say, the world was icy cold;
and for the Quileute, one winter was even worse than the rest.
Storm after storm ripped through their lands. Hail the size of rocks
hammered down, and blizzards battered their villages for days on
end. So terrible was the weather that they could not go hunting or
fishing, and they gradually began to starve.

At last the snow stopped falling, the ice began to melt, and the wind died
down a little. When the people emerged from their shelters,
they saw their villages wrecked and their lands laid waste, the plants
and trees all destroyed. How could they rebuild everything when they
were so weak with hunger? Filled with despair, they prayed to the
Great Spirit to help them.

As they looked out across the ocean, they saw huge dark clouds
gathering in the sky. They were horrified, fearing yet another terrible
storm. The sound of deep, loud thunder rumbled across the bay,
and flashes of lightning darted from the clouds. The people trembled
and wept, and some clung to one another in terror, while others ran
back to their shelters.

Soon the looming storm clouds were almost above the seashore
where the people stood, and the air shook with the booming thunder.
The sky was dark, lit only by spectacular lightning bolts. But, just as the
people were about to give up hope, the clouds in the sky drifted apart,

and the shape of a vast bird could be seen
emerging from the storm. Its wingspan was
as wide as the whole bay. Each of its feathers was the size
of one of their canoes. It was the Thunderbird himself.

The people fled, running to hide behind the pine trees
that lined the shore. They turned to see a sight of such wonder
that they could barely believe their eyes. Gripped tightly in
the Thunderbird's claws was a huge whale, plucked out of the
distant ocean. Deafening wingbeats echoed around the sky as he
flew closer, hovering above them. Then, the Thunderbird suddenly let
go of the whale, and it fell through the air, landing on the shore with
a great thud that shook the Earth.

Letting out an almighty screech, the Thunderbird flapped his wings,
turned around, and flew back up into the clouds. The storm drew
back across the ocean, the wind calmed, and the sound of thunder
faded into the distance.

The people went down to the beach where the dead whale lay.
They could not believe their luck. This one whale would give them
enough food to survive until the spring. They could replant their
crops, rebuild their homes, and start their lives again.

From that day on, the Quileute people worshiped the Thunderbird.
They carved his likeness at the top of their totem poles, to remind
all the generations to come of how the Thunderbird had saved
them. And whenever they heard rumbling thunder, or saw
lightning flash from the clouds, they knew that these were
nothing more than the beating of the Thunderbird's great
wings, and the blinking of his fire-filled eyes, and they
were no longer afraid.

ENCANTADO

Shapeshifting dolphin that
can change into a handsome man

An Encantado, meaning "enchanted," is a were-dolphin: a pink river dolphin that can transform itself into a man. According to Brazilian folklore, this happens when there's a full moon, and a festival or celebration going on. The Encantado loves music and dancing, so if he hears the sounds of a party, he shapeshifts into his human form and steps ashore.

The Encantado always appears as a handsome young man, dressed in elaborate, colorful clothes. No one seems to know him, but he charms everyone with his dancing and singing. He has a secret, though: even as a human, he still has a dolphin's blowhole on top of his head. He always covers it with his hat, which he refuses to take off.

Women often fall in love with the Encantado, not realizing his true nature. Encantados sometimes kidnap women, carrying them away to the Encante, their enchanted underwater home. Or a human woman and an Encantado may have a baby, which might be born with a blowhole or other dolphin-like features. One day, it will return to the river to join its father.

If an Encantado stays too late at a party, he risks turning back into a dolphin at dawn. He will begin running back toward the river, however much the other partygoers beg him to stay. Once or twice, people have reported seeing the handsome stranger reaching the riverbank by moonlight, and changing back into a dolphin as he plunges into the water.

RAVEN

*The shapeshifting, trick-playing,
fun-loving god of change*

On the Haida Gwaii islands in the Pacific Ocean live
the Haida people, who tell many stories of the spirit
animal Raven. A trickster and shapeshifter, Raven is always
causing trouble, yet he's also clever and kind. He loves
laughter, food, and fun, and, like all ravens and crows,
he collects interesting trinkets.

Raven plays tricks on and steals from the other gods and
spirit animals. But he does this out of curiosity, and to help
the humans. Raven gave humans water, which he stole from
Grey Eagle, and the art of housebuilding, stolen from the beaver.
In fact, Raven found the very first humans inside a clam shell,
and set them free. He also created Haida Gwaii, by dropping
stones into the sea; they stretched out and turned into islands.

Most famously of all, it was Raven who
brought light to the world, long, long ago…

RAVEN
UNLEASHES THE LIGHT

In the beginning, everything was dark. There was no Sun, Moon, or stars. Raven was annoyed by the darkness. He was tired of bumping into things and not knowing where he was going. He decided to do something about it.

Raven flew around the world, until he came to a small house where an old man lived with his daughter. As Raven passed by, he heard the old man say: "I have a box inside a box inside a box, and it holds all the light in the world. But no one will ever see it."

Raven was determined to steal the light. He flew down to the stream beside the house. When the young woman came out to collect water, he shapeshifted into a seed, and hid in her water jar. She drank from the jar, and swallowed the seed. It went down into her belly, and there Raven shapeshifted into a baby.

Soon, the woman gave birth to a little boy. The old man and his daughter were delighted with the baby, although he was a little strange. He was endlessly curious and wanted to play with everything. When he didn't get what he wanted, he shrieked loudly, like a bird. But they loved him, and as he grew older, they let him explore the house.

Disguised as the child, Raven searched everywhere for the box of light. Finally, he found a large box. The old man told him not to play with it, but Ravenchild shrieked, throwing a huge tantrum, until the grandfather said, "All right, you can play with the box. But don't open it!"

Well, you can imagine what happened next. Ravenchild opened the box, and found a smaller box inside. Again his grandfather told him not to play with it, and again Ravenchild shrieked until the old man's ears hurt. So he let the boy play with the second box. "But DON'T open it!" he warned.

But Ravenchild opened the second box, and inside he found the smallest box. "No!" cried his grandfather. "Not that box!" And he tried to take it, but Ravenchild shrieked until the old man was so exhausted, he gave in.

Now Ravenchild had the box containing all the light in the world. He opened it and pulled out a shining sphere of light. Before the old man could stop him, he shapeshifted back into a bird, and flew out of the window with the sphere of light in his beak.

Oh how happy Raven was, to be able to see everything at last! He flew across the sky, and all around him, mountains and forests, oceans, islands, and rivers were revealed for the first time. How beautiful they looked!

Just then, a huge eagle swooped toward him. He squawked in fear, and dropped the sphere of light. It fell to the ground, shattering into thousands of pieces, which flew up into the sky. The largest piece became the Sun, the second-largest piece became the Moon, and all the tiny pieces became the stars. Now there was light everywhere, even at night.

The old man and his daughter were sad to lose their little boy. But they could see their house, their stream, the beautiful mountains and forests, the sunrise, and the Moon and stars— and they began to feel better.

AUÑ PANA

Cunning and creepy
monster fish of the Amazon jungle

The Amazon rainforest has many deep, dark rivers, where mysterious creatures are said to lurk. According to the local Yanomami people, they include the most frightening fish-monsters you could imagine: the evil and merciless Auñ Pana.

Instead of scales, their bodies are covered in rough hair. Their large jaws are filled with long, sharp teeth, and, scariest of all, they have two long arms like a human's. They use these to grab anyone unlucky enough to fall into the water, before tearing them apart and devouring them in seconds.

The Auñ Pana are also clever and cunning. They plan ahead, dreaming up ways to lure or trick people into the water to become their next meal. And even if they don't end up eating their prey, they'll use their monstrous magic to spread chaos and disaster, destroying their victims in any way they can...

THE AUÑ PANA
AND THE BRIDGE

One day, a group of Yanomami people set off to go fishing. They came to the river, and began to cross the old wooden bridge, built by their ancestors many moons ago. But as they walked over it, something felt strange. There was an unfamiliar creaking sound, and the bridge seemed to tilt and shift. The people stopped, looking around in fear.

Below them, the evil Auñ Pana were lying in wait. In fact, they had been watching the Yanomami for weeks, learning where they went fishing, and when they crossed the bridge. Every night they had chewed at the wooden poles below the water, making them weaker and weaker. Now, at last, the poles were about to break, and the fearsome fish-monsters were ready to attack.

With a huge splash, the bridge collapsed into the river. The Yanomami tried to cling on, but one by one, they plunged into the water, where the hungry Auñ Pana grabbed them, dragged them underwater, and feasted on their flesh.

However, one part of the bridge had broken free, and floated off down the river, like a ramshackle raft. Several survivors were clinging to it, paddling as fast as they could to escape. But as the Auñ Pana finished their feeding frenzy, a long, hairy fish arm rose from the river and pointed downstream. One of the monsters had spotted the raft. And the Auñ Pana do not like to be outwitted.

The people paddled more furiously than ever, trying to reach the shore. But the shoal of monster fish surged down the river. Catching up with the raft, they surrounded it. The survivors stared in horror as the leader of the Auñ Pana raised his head out of the river and shrieked: "No one escapes the Auñ Pana!"

The poor people trembled with fear, expecting to be eaten alive. But the leader went on: "None of us can eat another thing. But you will still not escape. As punishment for trying to get away, you will become pigs and monkeys!" He flicked his tail to and fro, and, one by one, the people on the raft shrank and changed, becoming like the pigs and monkeys of the jungle. With that, the Auñ Pana sank beneath the surface and disappeared, and the raft drifted on down the river.

At last it came to rest on a muddy bank, and the pigs and monkeys ran ashore. Though they looked like animals, they were relieved to be alive, and longed to return to their village. They needed to tell the rest of their people what had happened, and warn them about the Auñ Pana. They made their way through the jungle, the monkeys swinging in the trees, the pigs snuffling along the ground. As they approached their village, they ran forward, desperate to tell their friends and relatives everything. In that moment, they forgot that they were pigs and monkeys.

But the villagers saw only wild animals, the ones they hunted and ate every day. They grabbed their blowpipes, unable to believe their luck. And so those unlucky last few survivors ended up being caught, then roasted on the fire and eaten for dinner that night, without ever being able to tell their terrible story.

EUROPE

From opposite ends of Europe come the great ancient Greek and Norse mythologies, which tell of magical, mysterious creatures. The lands between are also rich with dragons and other monsters of both land and sea.

PEGASUS

*Beautiful winged horse
of the ancient Greek gods*

In ancient Greek legends, Pegasus is a magical flying horse,
with huge, beautiful white-feathered wings. He lives on Mount
Olympus, the home of the gods. Athena, goddess of war and
wisdom, tamed Pegasus and cares for him.

Pegasus helps Zeus, the king of the gods, by carrying
the lightning and thunder Zeus uses as weapons. The other
gods often ride on Pegasus, and so do human heroes such
as Bellerophon, who caught Pegasus and rode him to fight
the monstrous, fire-breathing Chimera. Pegasus also created
the Hippocrene, an enchanted spring on Mount Helicon,
by stamping on the ground with his hoof. Anyone who drinks
from its waters is said to be blessed with poetic inspiration.

Perhaps surprisingly, this beautiful creature
is the son of the gorgon Medusa, a hideous
monster with snakes for hair...

THE BIRTH OF PEGASUS

In the east, on the remote, rocky island of Sarpedon, lived Medusa, a gorgon. Her hair was made of writhing venomous snakes that hissed and tangled themselves around her head. Her face was so frightening that anyone who looked at it was instantly turned to stone. Surrounding the cave where the gorgons lived were the crumbling statues of all the warriors and adventurers who had dared to approach Medusa, and had been petrified by her terrible glare.

Far away on the isle of Seriphos lived Perseus, a strong, brave young hero. He was the son of Danae, a human princess, and Zeus, the king of the gods. Polydectes, the king of Seriphos, decided he wanted to marry Danae. She didn't want to marry him, but because he was her king, it was difficult for her to refuse. She only had her son Perseus to protect her. To get him out of the way, Polydectes commanded Perseus to go to Sarpedon and bring him the head of Medusa. He was sure that Perseus would be turned to stone, and never seen again.

Looking down from Mount Olympus, Zeus saw what was happening, and sent the other gods to help Perseus with his task. Athena lent him a polished, shining shield, and Hermes lent him his winged sandals, which gave the wearer the power of flight. Hephaestus lent Perseus a razor-sharp sword, and Hades gave him a helmet that made the wearer invisible.

Wearing the magical sandals, Perseus flew to Sarpedon and soon found the gorgons' cave. Medusa was fast asleep inside. Perseus put on the helmet to make himself invisible. He crept toward Medusa, using the polished shield as a mirror to look only at her reflection. When he was close enough, he used the sword to slice off her head.

Then, to Perseus's astonishment, instead of blood, two magical creatures sprang out of Medusa's neck. One was a giant with a golden sword: the warrior Chrysaor. The other was a gleaming white horse that flew up into the air, flapping two enormous wings: the magical steed Pegasus. They were Medusa's children.

As Pegasus was born, a bolt of lightning crashed down and struck the island. Pegasus rose higher into the sky and flew away to live on Mount Olympus, where he became a loyal servant of the gods, carrying them far and wide on their many adventures. At last, when Pegasus died, Zeus transformed him into the Pegasus constellation in the night sky, which can still be seen today.

And what about Perseus? Well, he bundled Medusa's head into his backpack, out of sight, and flew back home to Seriphos. There, he went to find King Polydectes, who was more than a little alarmed to see him alive. Perseus pulled out the gorgon's head and presented it to the king, with its face toward him. As soon as he laid eyes upon it, Polydectes turned to stone, and Perseus and his mother, Danae, were free to live in happiness again.

CHIMERA

*Fire-breathing monster that's part lion,
part goat, and part serpent*

One of the deadliest monsters of Greek mythology, the Chimera
was a giant, fire-breathing beast. She had the head and body of a lion,
a goat's head on her back, and a venomous snake for a tail.

The Chimera was said to live in the mountainous land
of Lycia, where she terrorized the whole country, destroying villages
and farms with her fiery breath. To see her, even if you were
lucky enough to survive the encounter, was an omen that a
disaster, such as a killer volcanic eruption, was coming.

Many heroes tried to kill this formidable creature, but
it seemed an impossible task. As soon as they came close
enough to attack her, she killed them with a jet of flame.

However, in one story, King Iobates of Lycia asked the hero
Bellerophon to get rid of the Chimera for him. To help Bellerophon,
the goddess Athena agreed that Pegasus, the winged horse
of the gods, could carry him to Lycia.

Bellerophon prepared for the attack by fixing a lump
of lead to the tip of his spear. He flew high above
the monster on Pegasus's back, so that the flames
could not reach him, and took aim. He hurled
the spear at the Chimera's gaping mouth.
As it plunged into her throat, her breath
melted the lead, choking her to death.

CERBERUS

*Fierce three-headed
guard dog of the underworld*

In ancient Greek legends, when people die, they go
down to the dark, shadowy underworld. It's ruled over
by Hades, the god of the dead, and guarding the
entrance is Cerberus, his loyal hound.

Cerberus is the son of two monsters, Typhon and Echidna,
and he is no ordinary dog. He is enormous, with a black,
shaggy coat that has venomous snakes growing out of it,
a snake's tail, and lion's claws. Some stories say he has
a hundred heads, some fifty—but in most legends he has
three heads, each with long, jagged teeth dripping with
poisonous drool. When dead souls arrive at the underworld,
Cerberus greets them like a friendly puppy. But if anyone ever
tries to leave, or to enter the underworld without permission,
he tears them apart and devours them in seconds.

It is possible, however, to overcome
Cerberus—if you know how...

CERBERUS
AND HERACLES

O nly three people have ever managed to overpower Cerberus, the three-headed dog who guards the deep, dark underworld.

One was Orpheus, who wanted to rescue his lost wife, Eurydice, from the underworld. He played such a beautiful lullaby on his lyre that Cerberus began to sleep, enabling Orpheus to sneak past. The second was the Sibyl of Cumae, a powerful priestess. When Aeneas wanted to enter the underworld to visit his dead father, the priestess helped him by feeding Cerberus a honey cake containing herbs that drugged the dog into a deep slumber.

The third was Heracles. He was the son of Zeus, half-human, half-god, with extraordinary courage and strength. To become immortal, Heracles had to complete twelve tasks set by King Eurystheus of Tiryns. They were known as the twelve labors of Heracles, and most of them involved killing or capturing dangerous monsters. The twelfth and final task was to go to the underworld and catch Cerberus, then bring him back to King Eurystheus alive. Of course, King Eurytheus was sure this could not be done.

Athena, the goddess of war and wisdom, and Hermes, the messenger of the gods, helped Heracles by showing him a secret hidden entrance to the underworld, which was not guarded by Cerberus. Entering it, Heracles found King Hades himself, who was astonished and impressed to see a living man before him. When Heracles said he had come to capture Cerberus, Hades granted him permission to try. "But," he said, "you may not use any weapons, only your bare hands." Hades did not want his beloved dog to be harmed.

Heracles traveled through the underworld to the gates where Cerberus stood watch. He crept up behind the huge hound, watching as the snakes in his fur hissed and writhed. But Heracles was wearing the skin of the Nemean lion, a vicious beast that he had killed as the first of his tasks. Its skin could not be penetrated by any weapon, tooth, or blade.

Heracles grabbed Cerberus around his three necks, holding him as tightly as he could. Cerberus's three heads growled and snapped, and the venomous snakes bit Heracles, but the lion's skin protected him. At last, Cerberus grew weaker, struggling to breathe. He sank down in the hero's arms, exhausted, and let Heracles chain him and drag him away from the underworld, up toward the light of day.

As Heracles led Cerberus to the land of Tiryns to bring him to King Eurystheus, the bright sunlight made the poor dog sick. He drooled and vomited, and wherever the drops landed, deadly poisonous wolfsbane plants grew. You can still find them across Greece to this day.

At last Heracles brought Cerberus to King Eurystheus. The king was so horrified to see the hound of Hades himself, he ran away and hid in a large bronze jar. From inside it, he pleaded, "Please, Heracles, take Cerberus back home! You have completed your task!"

So that is what Heracles did. He knew Cerberus had an important job to do, and was missing his home and his master, Hades. So he led the hound all the way back, and released him into the underworld again, where he has stayed ever since.

ZILANT

*Fierce, fire-breathing,
fast-flying dragon*

The Zilants are dangerous two-legged dragons from the
folklore of eastern Europe and western Russia. Part snake
and part bird, Zilants have a long, serpentine tail and chicken's
claws and fly fast on their bright red wings. But a Zilant's head
is all dragon, with scales, horns, and a long, pointed tongue,
as well as flames shooting from its nostrils.

The most famous Zilant of all is the Zilant of Kazan. In ancient
times, the Khan of Kazan decided to move his city to Zilantlaw
Hill. The hill was infested with snakes, so the khan had them
killed to make way for the new buildings. The leader of the snakes
was a deadly Zilant, which escaped and vowed to take revenge.
He hid in a cave, flying out only to drink the water of Kazan's
Black Lake and to attack its inhabitants. This terrifying
Zilant became the subject of many legends...

The Princess
and the Zilant

Long, long ago, a powerful princess ruled the city of Kazan. She was a brave warrior, and her archery skills were admired across the land. However, a great army from the east was sweeping through Russia and Europe, and Kazan was in danger.

Many of the princess's soldiers had died in battle, and her army was too small to fight off the invaders. She needed help. So she called her chief advisor, and said: "Go and seek out the fierce Zilant who lives in the cave on the hill, and ask him to come and see me."

The advisor thought the princess must be crazy. Everyone knew the Zilant was an evil dragon who flew around gobbling people up. But he went to the cave and asked the Zilant if he would come to meet the princess. To his surprise, the Zilant agreed, and followed the advisor to the castle, where the princess was waiting.

"Thank you, mighty Zilant, for coming to see me," the princess began. "I need your help. Invaders from the east are approaching, and we cannot compete with them. Will you guard the city?"

The Zilant thought for a minute, and then answered: "I will help you. But I require payment."

"What payment?" asked the princess.

The Zilant answered, "I need a constant supply of food, including plenty of fresh grass, and a child and a woman every three weeks."

"Agreed," said the princess.

Satisfied with the deal, the Zilant set off to guard the city. He built himself a nest from chains, suspended from a tall oak tree, and curled up inside it for a nap.

The poor princess was in turmoil. She had to agree to the Zilant's demands, but she could not sacrifice her people. She had three weeks to see off the invaders and somehow get rid of the Zilant too.

The Zilant was lying in his nest when he heard the sound of hooves, and thought the invading army had arrived. He flew out of his nest like an arrow on fire. But as he swooped down, he saw a scruffy man on a tired-looking old horse, leading a band of knights.

The Zilant was confused. "Is this the enemy?" he wondered. "Surely not! He's not scary at all!" He flew closer, lowering his neck to take a closer look. As he did so, the peasant whipped out his sword and sliced the dragon's head off.

The Zilant had been right—this was not the invading army. The man was Gol, a poor peasant, who had persuaded the knights to follow him by boasting that he was a great fighter. When he saw the dragon, Gol thought he was doomed. But he grabbed the chance to kill the Zilant and save his own life.

The princess was so impressed, she invited Gol and his knights into her castle. She sent for a bottle of Water of Heroes, a magical medicine that she drank every day. She gave some to Gol, and he became a brave warrior. With Gol and his knights, the princess fought off the invaders and saved the city of Kazan.

BASILISK

Small but deadly serpent king

Ancient Roman and medieval legends tell of the most
feared of all beasts, the lethal Basilisk. Half-reptile,
half-bird, it has the tail of a snake, but its front
end resembles a cockerel, with a beak, feathers,
and two legs for crawling. It also has two scaly
wings, similar to a dragon's.

Basilisks are created when a cockerel sits on a snake's egg
until it hatches, and the deadly creature emerges.
They are quite small, but extremely dangerous. A Basilisk
has a deadly gaze, and anyone who looks into its eyes will
drop dead on the spot. It is also so venomous that touching it
means instant death. Even if a knight on horseback touches
a Basilisk with his spear, the venom will travel up the
spear and kill both man and horse. Lastly, Basilisks have
evil breath, which will poison you if you breathe it in.

As the Basilisk crawls along, plants wither and die,
and the ground is left bare and scorched. Other animals flee,
especially birds and snakes, which fear it above all else.

There are ways to defeat a Basilisk, however.
One animal, the lowly weasel, is immune to its weapons,
and its urine emits an odor that kills this venomous beast.

Alternatively, use the Basilisk's own powers to
kill it by showing it a mirror. If it sees its reflection,
it will die at once from the sight of its own face.

KRAKEN

Many-tentacled monster of the deep

Since medieval times, fishermen and sailors have told stories of a gargantuan, deadly sea creature: the terrifying Kraken. This monstrous beast, said to roam the seas between Iceland and Norway, has a huge head, enormous eyes, and long, sucker-covered tentacles—similar to an octopus or squid, but many times the size. Some say it's the length of ten ships. Others say it's over a mile long!

The Kraken is said to spend most of its time at the bottom of the ocean, where it devours its favorite food, large shoals of fish. But, once in a while, it ventures up to the sea surface. If disturbed by a passing ship, it wraps its tentacles right around to drag the ship beneath the waves, drowning everyone on board.

Often, though, the Kraken simply snoozes, floating peacefully in the water. As they pass by, seafarers sometimes mistake its barnacle-covered bulk for a small island. They go ashore to explore, and perhaps set up camp. But if they make the mistake of lighting a campfire, the creature will suddenly wake up. Roaring in pain, it will plunge down into the depths, creating a powerful whirlpool that sucks the sailors and their ship under the waves with it.

RATATOSKR

Troublemaking, rumor-spreading
red squirrel of the world-tree

In the Norse mythology of northern Scandinavia, the universe
is held together by a huge ash tree, whose name is Yggdrasil.
Among its roots lives the dragon Nidhoggr, who chews on the bodies
of the dead. And at the top, in the highest branches, lives a great
eagle, who flaps his wings to make the winds blow on Earth.

Now, this mighty eagle and Nidhoggr the dragon hate each other,
and always have. Since they live at opposite ends of Yggdrasil,
that wouldn't be a problem—if it weren't for Ratatoskr. Ratatoskr
is a mischievous red squirrel who spends his days scampering up
and down the tree, carrying messages between the dragon
at the bottom and the eagle at the top.

But these aren't useful messages—they are just gossip and lies,
spread by the squirrel to stir up trouble. If Nidhoggr complains about
the eagle, Ratatoskr runs up and passes the insults on, perhaps adding
a few of his own. When the eagle gets angry and curses Nidhoggr,
Ratatoskr runs straight back down, to whisper
his rude words into the dragon's ears.

In this way, the scurrilous squirrel has his fun, ensuring
there's always a fight going on. In fact, some say
Ratatoskr would like to destroy Yggdrasil. Unable
to do so on his own, he enrages the dragon and the
eagle so that they gnaw at the roots and tear off the
branches. That's why, thanks to Ratatoskr, Yggdrasil
and the universe itself are never at peace.

FENRIR

Monstrous wolf of Asgard, land of the gods

Fenrir is one of the most terrifying creatures in all of Norse mythology. He is a giant, ferocious wolf, with enormous razor-sharp teeth in his huge slobbering jaws, and claws like steel blades. Even the strongest and bravest of the gods are nervous when they see Fenrir—and not just because of his size and fearsome bite.

Fenrir is no ordinary wolf. His father is Loki, the troublemaking trickster god, and his mother is the giantess Angrboda. A terrible prophecy foretold that Fenrir would one day devour Odin, the king of the gods, and swallow the Sun itself, when Ragnarok, the end of the world, finally arrived. Hoping to avoid this fate, the gods decided to bring Fenrir to live with them in their homeland, Asgard, to raise him themselves, and keep a close eye on him…

FENRIR IN CHAINS

When Fenrir first came to Asgard, he was little more than a wolf cub. But he was still so fierce that only Tyr, the brave god of justice, dared to feed him. The gods soon noticed that the wolf was growing at an alarming rate. Before long, he would be too big to control. They needed a way to restrain Fenrir, to make sure he could not cause trouble.

So they forged a set of massive metal chains, so heavy that even Thor, the mighty god of thunder, could barely lift them. Then the gods called: "Fenrir, will you come here and help us with something?"
    The wolf ran over to them.

"We need to see how strong these chains are," Thor said. "You must be the strongest creature in Asgard. Will you test them to see if you can break free?" Fenrir liked a challenge, so he let Thor tie him up. Then, with an almost effortless stretch, he broke free, snapping the metal easily.

The gods were dismayed to discover just how strong Fenrir was. They went back to their workshop and built an even bigger, thicker set of chains, so heavy that it took several gods to lift them. Again, they called Fenrir, and he bounded toward them.

"We think these might be the strongest chains in the world," Thor said. "Will you help us test them again?" Fenrir agreed, so the gods tied him up, confident that the new chains could restrain him. They were wrong. Within a few moments, the wolf had broken free.

This time, Odin himself had a plan. He sent a messenger to Svartalfheim, the home of the elves, to ask them to make an unbreakable chain. A few days later, they sent back their handiwork— but it was nothing more than a fine, silky ribbon. The elves explained that this chain, called Gleipnir, was made from six ingredients:

- The sound of a cat's footsteps
- The roots of a mountain
- The beard of a woman
- The sinews of a bear
- The breath of a fish
- The spittle of a bird

Since these things were impossible to obtain, they said, Gleipnir would be impossible to break.

Again the gods asked Fenrir to test their new chain. But when he saw the fine ribbon, he was suspicious. "If that ribbon is strong enough to hold me," he said, "there must be magic involved. Are you trying to trick me?"

"No, we promise," said Odin. "And if this ribbon can hold you, then we'll know you are not a danger, and we'll set you free."

"I'll do it, on one condition," said Fenrir. "One of you must put your hand in my mouth while I test it." The gods looked at one another. They knew that if Fenrir were trapped, he would bite the hand off. But brave Tyr stepped forward and put his hand between the wolf's massive jaws. Then the gods tied Fenrir up.

Fenrir flexed his muscles, thinking the ribbon would break, but it didn't. He kicked and strained and pulled, but Gleipnir just grew stronger and tighter. Growling in anger, Fenrir bit Tyr's hand off at the wrist. Tyr screamed in pain—but to everyone's relief, the wolf was finally held fast. For now, at least…

AFRICA

*Africa's many cultures and peoples have countless tales
of mythical beings, from the animal-headed Egyptian gods of the north,
to fearsome beasts like South Africa's Grootslang. And it's only thanks
to the spider god Anansi that the world has stories at all...*

ANANSI

*West African spider god,
trickster, and bringer of stories*

In West Africa, there are countless stories about
Anansi the spider. He is no ordinary spider, although
he sometimes looks like one. Anansi is a shapeshifting
trickster god, who might sometimes appear as a man with
a many-eyed head, a man with eight legs, or a spider with
a human face. His mother is Asase Yaa, the Earth
goddess, and his father is Nyame, the sky god.

Wise and clever, Anansi is a master storyteller. He uses his wit and
stories to trick others into doing what he wants, often succeeding
at tasks that seem impossible. Anansi can cause mischief, but he
also helps people by showing them how to overcome problems
using wisdom and cunning. He often persuades his father,
Nyame, to give things to the humans, such as the rain.
And it was Anansi who brought stories to humans
in the first place, when they had none...

ANANSI AND THE
BOX OF STORIES

As Anansi the spider looked around at the world, he realized something was missing. There were no stories! The people had no tales to tell one another around the fire at night. Anansi's father, the sky god Nyame, was keeping them all to himself, locked inside a box in his kingdom in the heavens. Anansi decided to get the box, and give the stories to the world.

He spun a long thread of silk, and climbed up to the heavens to talk to Nyame. "Great Nyame," he said, "I have come to ask you for the box of stories."

"Hmmm," said Nyame. "You can have the box, but only if you can catch three things and bring them to me. They are Onini the python, Osebo the leopard, and Mboro the swarm of hornets."

As Nyame knew, these creatures were all extremely dangerous and difficult to catch. He was sure Anansi would fail. But Anansi was determined.

First, he approached Onini, the giant python. While holding a large stick, he said to himself: "Oh no, she must be wrong. I'm sure Onini is longer than this!"

"What are you talking about?" asked the python, turning to see Anansi. "Oh, hello Onini," he said. "It's just that my wife says you're not as long as this stick."

"Of COURSE I am!" Onini hissed.

"But how can I prove it?" Anansi sighed. "I know! You lie alongside the stick, and I'll measure you."

Keen to prove his great length, the python stretched out next to the stick. Quick as a flash, Anansi spun his silk around them both, holding Onini tight.

"You tricked me!" groaned Onini, as Anansi pulled him up to the heavens to show Nyame.

Next, Anansi found Osebo, the fierce leopard. Standing behind her, he said: "How can they say that about Osebo? Surely she's the cleverest animal in the forest."

"How can they say WHAT about me?" Osebo growled, turning to see Anansi holding a large sack. "Oh, hello Osebo," Anansi said. "It's just that people are saying you're not clever enough to squeeze into this sack."

"What nonsense," said Osebo. "Of course I can." She sprang from the rock into the sack. Anansi quickly spun his silk around it, tying it tight.

"You tricked me, Anansi!" Osebo roared, as Anansi hauled her up to the heavens.

Finally, Anansi filled a large pot with water, and poured it all over the hornets' nest.

"What's going on?" buzzed the hornets from inside. "Is it rainy season already?"

"Don't worry!" said Anansi. "I've brought you this pot to shelter in."

"Oh, thank you, spider!" said the hornets, flying into the pot. At once, Anansi spun his silk over the opening, sealing it tight.

"You tricked us!" the hornets cried from inside the pot, as Anansi carried it up to the heavens.

Nyame had to admit defeat. "Well done, little spider," he said. He handed Anansi a small, simple wooden box, and when Anansi lifted the lid, out spilled all the stories, tumbling down to the ground below and spreading to every land. And now the world is full of stories, thanks to Anansi the spider.

GROOTSLANG

Terrifying, cave-dwelling, elephant–snake hybrid

Hideous, cunning, and as old as the world itself, the Grootslang is a very strange creature indeed. According to South African folklore, the gods made the Grootslang by mistake, when they were new to creating animals and had not had enough practice. The beast that resulted was a half-elephant, half-snake monster, highly intelligent, incredibly strong, and horribly cruel.

When the gods saw what they had done, they decided to split snakes and elephants into two separate, and slightly less dangerous, animal families. But the first Grootslang escaped and hid in a deep cave in the region of Richtersveld, where it's still said to live to this day. Locals call the cave the Wonder Hole or the Bottomless Pit. A terrible smell drifts from its gloomy entrance, and few people dare to go near it.

Despite being half-elephant itself, the Grootslang lures elephants into its lair, where it attacks and eats them. It will also feed on other animals, and humans too, if it can. It has one weakness, though—it adores diamonds and precious stones, and has a hoard of them inside its cave, which it guards jealously. If you're ever about to be devoured by the Grootslang, you may be able to save yourself by offering it a diamond or gemstone in exchange for your life.

NYAMI NYAMI

Powerful river god of the Zambezi

In southeastern Africa, the mighty Zambezi River flows between the lands of Zambia and Zimbabwe. The local Tonga people, who live along the shores of the Zambezi, have always paid their respects to the great Nyami Nyami, the god of the river. He is sometimes described as a giant serpent with the head of a fierce, sharp-toothed fish. Others say he is more like a huge water-dragon, or a spiral-shaped creature resembling a whirlwind. They say his snake-like body is at least ten feet thick, the height of a single-story house. But how long he is, no one has ever dared to guess.

Along with his wife, another water monster, Nyami Nyami patrols the Zambezi, guarding its wildlife and controlling its waters. Long ago, he was said to dwell in a deep gorge, below a rock named Kariwa, meaning "trap." Anyone who paddled their canoe too close would be sucked underwater, never to return. And if the river god was angry, he could cause floods and storms. But he also helped the Tonga people, providing them with food in times of need.

After a dam was built across the river many years ago, Nyami Nyami's deep valley was transformed into a large lake, and Kariwa, the rock marking his home, was submerged. Some say he still swims around in the lake to this day, shaking his tail with a loud rumble, and making the dam and the riverbanks tremble.

OLITIAU

*Scary, super-sized, bat-like beast
of the African rainforest*

In the humid rainforests of central Africa, people speak
of a terrifying, giant, bat-like creature, the Olitiau. Its name
is taken from ceremonial masks used to represent demons,
and it has long been regarded as a dangerous monster.

In a famous eyewitness account from 1932, two European explorers
described how they were wading in a stream in Cameroon when they
saw a vast bat swooping down at them. They ducked to avoid it,
but had time to see the creature close-up. It had a flattened face,
similar to an ape's, and its lower jaw hung open, revealing sharp,
two-inch-long white teeth. And its huge wingspan looked about 13
feet long—which would make it more than twice as big as any bat on
record. When they told the locals about it, all agreed it was an Olitiau.

Perhaps the explorers had come across a new species of giant bat,
so far unknown to science. It's even been suggested that the Olitiau
could be a flying reptile, similar to a pterodactyl, that   has survived
in the forest since the age of the dinosaurs. But   sightings
are so rare, no one knows for sure.

ANUBIS

Jackal-headed god of death and mummification

In ancient Egyptian myths, Anubis is one of
the most important gods. He is the god of death
and embalming—the process of making dead bodies into
mummies, so that they can enter the afterlife. Anubis also
guides the souls of the dead to Duat, the Egyptian underworld.

Before a soul can enter the afterlife, Anubis helps Osiris, his father
and the god of the underworld, to weigh its heart. The heart
is balanced against a feather on a set of golden scales. If the
heart is lighter than the feather, the person has done good deeds,
and may proceed to the afterlife. But if the heart is heavier,
it is eaten by Ammut, a crocodile goddess.

Anubis appears as a black jackal (a type of wild dog),
or as a man with a jackal's head. It was in his man
form that he invented embalming…

ANUBIS MAKES
THE FIRST MUMMY

At first, Anubis was the ruler of Duat, the underworld, where he watched over dead souls in the afterlife. That changed after the death of his father, Osiris, when Anubis invented embalming and the making of mummies.

In the beginning, Geb, god of the Earth, and Nut, god of the sky, created four great gods: Osiris, Isis, Set, and Nephthys. As the first to be created, Osiris became the ruler of the world, with Isis as his wife. Set, the god of chaos and disorder, was Osiris's brother, and his wife was Nephthys. But Nephthys preferred Osiris, so she disguised herself as Isis. Osiris, believing she was his wife, had a child with her. That baby was Anubis.

Nephthys was frightened that Set might find out what she had done, so she hid Anubis in the marshes next to the River Nile. Realizing what had happened, Isis went and found the baby, and raised him as her own.

Set was furious with Osiris when he found out, and jealous of his power as ruler of the world. He swore that one day he would kill Osiris and take his throne, and eventually he did. He tricked Osiris into climbing inside a wooden chest, then sealed it shut and threw it into the Nile. Osiris floated away down the river and out to sea. Set, as he had planned, took his brother's place as ruler of the world.

Isis, Osiris's wife, searched everywhere for the chest, and finally found it far across the sea in the city of Byblos, where it had washed ashore. She brought Osiris's body home to Egypt, then went to prepare some magical herbs to try to bring him back to life. But before she could return, Set found the body. He chopped it into pieces and threw them all over Egypt, so that Osiris could never be alive again.

Isis, together with Anubis and Nephthys, traveled all over Egypt, collecting the body parts. But they could not find every single piece, meaning that Osiris could not come back to the world of the living. He had to go and live in Duat, the underworld, and become its ruler instead of Anubis.

To help his father become the ruler of Duat, Anubis prepared his body. He fitted all the pieces they had found back together. He dried out the body, and preserved it by coating it with oil, perfumes, and spices. He wrapped it in many layers of linen bandages, making the first mummy. In this way, Anubis ensured that Osiris's body would last forever, so that he could live in the afterlife as its ruler.

But Set was still causing trouble. He disguised himself as a leopard, and tried to steal Osiris's body. Anubis grabbed him and hit him all over with a red-hot iron rod, burning his skin with black marks. That is why leopards have black spots today. After that, Anubis tore off the leopard skin, and wore it himself as a cloak.

From then on, Anubis became the god of death and mummification, guarding over the process of preparing bodies for the next life, and guiding the souls of the dead to take their place there.

BASTET

*Graceful, protective goddess of cats,
women, and motherhood*

Bastet is the beloved cat goddess of ancient Egypt, appearing
as a cat, or as a woman with a cat's head. Like any feline, she has
a calm, affectionate side, but can also fight fiercely, especially
to protect her kittens. In this form, she becomes Sekhmet,
who has the head of a lion. She carries an ankh, the symbol
of life, or a sistrum, a kind of rattle.

The daughter of Ra, the great Sun god, Bastet is often shown
with the eye of Ra, the red disk of the Sun, above her head.
She has many important roles. She protects Ra himself, as
well as all the pharaohs of Egypt. She is the guardian of
women, and goddess of the home, family, and
motherhood. The mother of all domestic cats,
she protects the home from disease and evil, just
as a pet cat protects it from mice, rats, and snakes.
That is why she is called upon
in times of need…

BASTET, RA, AND APEP

Ra was the Sun god, the greatest of all gods, creator of the universe, bringer of life, and ruler of the three worlds: the underworld, the Earth, and the sky. Yet even with all his power, Ra was always in danger, and relied on others, especially his daughter Bastet, to help him survive.

Every day, Ra traveled across the sky to light up the world. He rose in the east, and made his way through the heavens in a boat named Mandjet, the Morning-boat, also known as the Boat of Millions of Years. But in the evening, as night fell, Ra had to travel below the horizon in the west, and journey through the underworld in a second boat, Mesektet, the Night-boat. All night he struggled in the darkness to find his way along the rivers of the underworld, back to the east, where he could rise once more and start a new day.

This was far from a simple task, for in these rivers lived Apep, the terrifying giant serpent, god of destruction and evil. Some say Apep had himself once been the ruler of the Universe, but had been overthrown by Ra. Others say he had formed soon after Ra's birth, but had become evil, forcing Ra to trap him in the underworld. There, his roars rumbled through the world as thunder, and his twisting and slithering caused earthquakes.

Wherever Apep had come from, he was angry, cruel, and determined to kill Ra. Every night, he chased and hunted the Sun god through the darkness, hoping to swallow him, as a snake swallows an egg on Earth. Apep had a magical, mesmerizing gaze, which he used to hypnotize Ra, slowing him down. But luckily Ra had helpers to protect him.

At first, Set, the god of chaos, would travel with Ra to guard him against Apep. The great serpent's hypnotizing eyes had no effect on Set, and he used his spear to stab and slash at Apep and fend him off. Despite this, Apep did manage to swallow the Sun occasionally, resulting in a solar eclipse. But Set would cut Ra out and set him free.

However, Ra grew tired of Set, because he always boasted about his snake-fighting skills and threatened to block out Ra's light with storms if he didn't praise him enough. To replace Set, Ra took his daughter Bastet, the cat goddess, on his journeys through the underworld. In her cat form, she fought off the serpent each night, saving Ra so that the next day could dawn.

In the end, it was Bastet who killed Apep once and for all. Cats, as everyone knows, have excellent night vision, and Bastet used her cat eyes to hunt the serpent down and creep up on him. She killed him by slicing his head off with a knife, held in her paw.

After killing Apep, Bastet was at last freed from her nightly task in the underworld. She returned to Earth to become the goddess of women and motherhood, and protector of the home. That is why the ancient Egyptians adored and worshiped cats, keeping them as pets to bring the spirit, strength, and protection of the goddess Bastet into their homes.

ASIA

This vast continent is home to hundreds of different peoples who have given us a wealth of stories and legends, featuring dragons and unicorns, monstrous birds, and Japan's supernatural Yokai.

ROC

Enormous, elephant-eating bird of prey

The mythologies of Arabia and Persia tell of the Rocs, giant birds of prey so huge that a single bird blocks out the Sun as it flies overhead. A Roc is said to look like an eagle, but much bigger—just one of its feathers is 12 human paces long. It has a forked tongue like a snake's, and talons so strong they can grasp and pick up an elephant, a Roc's favorite food.

The home of the Rocs is a secret valley, filled with precious stones. In the Arabian tales of Sinbad the sailor, Sinbad was washed ashore on a remote island, where he found a Roc's enormous egg. When the Roc arrived, Sinbad tied himself to its leg, and was carried away to the mysterious valley. He saw merchants standing on the cliffs around the valley, throwing down chunks of meat. The Rocs picked up the meat and carried it up to their nests, where the merchants collected the jewels that had stuck to it. Cunning Sinbad tied a piece of meat to his back. When a Roc picked up the meat, Sinbad was able to escape the valley, taking with him enough jewels to make his fortune.

RAINBOW FISH

Enormous, greedy fish of Hindu legend

According to ancient Hindu mythology, the massive, multicolored Rainbow Fish once swam the waters of the world. This fabulous fish was covered in sparkling scales in four different colors. Her green scales were made of grass, and symbolized the Earth. She also had yellow scales, made of lightning and evoking the air. Her red scales were made of flames, a tribute to the element of fire. Lastly, she had blue scales made of ice that embodied water.

The Rainbow Fish was as big as the biggest whale, and she swam all around the seas and oceans, always hungry and searching for food. One day, she saw a light shining on the surface of the water, and swam straight toward it to gobble it up. She swallowed it in one massive gulp, but little did she realize that she had eaten none other than golden-skinned, peace-loving Buddha, one of the many avatars, or forms, of the great god Vishnu.

The people could not allow one of the most important gods to be eaten by a fish. They had no choice but to rescue him. So the fishermen chased and caught the Rainbow Fish, and cut her open to free Vishnu from her stomach. Although the Rainbow Fish was sadly no more, her body was so enormous that there was enough fish for everyone in the country to live on for a whole year.

YETI

*Hairy, humanoid creature
of the snowy Himalayas*

The Yeti is one of the best-known legendary creatures,
yet also one of the most mysterious. A tall, strong, shaggy-haired,
human-shaped beast, it's said to live on the snowy slopes
of the Himalayan mountains in central Asia.

The Yeti is found in ancient folk tales, and reported
sightings of it date back more than a thousand years.
Some local legends describe it as a dangerous monster
that eats humans, with anyone who sees it becoming
weak and helpless. Others say it's a helpful spirit,
who guards the mountains, scaring away evil with
its glowing eyes and bloodcurdling shriek.

Many explorers have journeyed to the Himalayas in search
of the Yeti. Some have claimed to see it for themselves.
Others have found giant footprints, or seen skulls,
fur, or even droppings said to be the Yeti's.

Some think the Yeti is really a type of bear. Bears can
have very big feet, and some are known to stand upright
on their hind legs like a human. Or it might be a type of
giant ape, long thought to be extinct, but surviving in the
remote mountains. The high Himalayas are so hard
to explore that we may never truly know
if the Yeti is really out there.

FENGHUANG

Mysterious, beautiful bird of peace and happiness

Since the most ancient times, the Chinese have revered the mythical, magical Fenghuang. This legendary bird can be seen all over China, in carvings and statues, as jewelry, and on pottery and fabrics, from thousands of years ago to the present.

Sometimes called the Chinese phoenix, the giant Fenghuang is actually a combination of many other birds. It has the body of a duck, a beak like a parrot's, and a peacock's long, colorful tail. It also has long legs like a crane, and a swallow's wings. To top it all off, the Fenghuang's feathers are red, black, yellow, green, and white, and it is sometimes shown with a ball of fire, because it is said to have come from the Sun. On Earth, however, its home is the Kunlun mountains in northern China.

The ruler of all birds, the Fenghuang is a symbol of beauty, loyalty, happiness, and great leadership. According to legend, it would often appear at the start of a new era, when a king or queen was crowned, as an omen of peace and success. It could also be seen in times of prosperity and good fortune, but when it disappeared, there were hard times ahead.

Long ago, the Fenghuang was two birds, the Feng and the Huang, one male and one female. Today they are combined into one. That's why the Fenghuang is used as a symbol of good luck at weddings, and also represents the marriage of an emperor and an empress.

SHENLONG

*Blue-scaled Chinese dragon
of the clouds, wind, and rain*

In some countries, dragons are seen as fearsome monsters.
But the dragon, or "Long," of Chinese mythology is a majestic,
helpful, and much-loved creature. Dragons help humans
by sending them good weather to help their crops grow,
and protecting their ships at sea.

There are many types of dragon in Chinese legends, including
the Tianlong, guardian of the heavens, and the Dilong, ruler
of seas and rivers. Shenlong, the Spirit Dragon, is one of the most
important of all. He has power over the winds and clouds,
and brings the rain that is essential for growing rice.

Shenlong is covered in shimmering blue scales,
making him hard to spot as he floats through the sky.
Like other Chinese dragons, he has a long, snake-
like body, large horns and claws, and big, bulging
eyes. It's important to respect Shenlong and
keep him happy, otherwise the life-giving
rains might not arrive...

THE DRAGON PEARL

A young boy lived with his mother on the edge of a village. The people in the village were poor and made their living growing rice and vegetables. One day, the boy was gathering wood when he spotted a small red stone on the forest floor. It was polished and beautiful, and felt heavy in his hand. He took it home and hid it in the rice store for safe-keeping. Little did he know that he had found a dragon pearl.

The next morning, he went to fetch some rice from the store. It had been almost empty, but now it was overflowing. The boy saw his red stone in the middle. He took the stone and put it in the jar where his mother kept a few coins. When he went back, the jar was full of money. He ran to tell his mother what had happened. They could not believe their luck!

The boy knew that his neighbors were poor too. So he took the red stone and went around the village, filling up everyone's rice containers and money jars. The villagers were delighted that they no longer had to live in poverty.

But there was one problem. It had stopped raining. The wells were drying out, and the rice crops were dying. The boy tried putting his stone into a water bucket, but it sucked all the water away, and made it disappear.

"We can't live without water!" thought the boy. So he decided to go and find Shenlong the rain dragon, to ask him for rain. Soon after setting off, the boy met a snake, trapped under a rock. "Do you know where I can find Shenlong the rain dragon?" he asked the snake. The snake agreed to help him if he lifted the rock off his back, which the boy did.

"Go east," said the snake. Then he gave the boy some of his scales, telling him: "You will need these."

The boy headed east, eventually coming across an eagle with a broken wing. He asked if the bird knew where to find Shenlong.

"I will tell you if you mend my wing," said the eagle. So the boy made a splint from some twigs, and bandaged the wing. "Keep going east," said the eagle. "And take these claws."

Farther east, the boy came to a forest, where a stag stood with its antlers trapped between two trees.

"I'm looking for Shenlong the rain dragon," said the boy.

"I can help you, if you help me," said the stag. So the boy cut away the tree bark until the deer was free.

Then the stag removed his antlers and gave them to the boy, saying, "Keep heading east, and take these with you."

The boy journeyed on, finally arriving at an eastern shore. Feeling hot and tired, he ran into the sea. Then something strange happened. The snake's scales spread across his body. The claws grew on his fingers and toes. He felt the antlers on his head. The boy had become a rain dragon himself.

Leaping into the air, he flew back across the land until he reached his own village. He danced across the sky, showering the fields and crops with fresh, cool raindrops, until the wells were full and the villagers were saved.

QILIN

Kind and gentle unicorn-like beast,
famed for its power and goodness

A Qilin, pronounced "Chia-lin," is a strange and wonderful, horse-like being of Chinese mythology. Its body resembles a horse or a deer, but is covered in glittering green scales that sometimes glow with flames. Atop its head sit two horns, although sometimes it has only one, which is why some people call it the "Chinese unicorn." Unlike that of a typical unicorn, however, its horn is not twisted, but branched like a stag's. Its voice is like tinkling bells or chimes, and hearing it brings good luck.

A Qilin has great power, but is also the kindest, most peaceful of creatures. It treads so carefully that it can walk on grass without damaging a single blade, but, because it is reluctant to harm any living thing, it usually walks on water instead, or on the clouds high in the sky. Qilins never eat animals or even living plants, feeding only on a special magical grass.

Among its other abilities, a Qilin can tell if a person is good or bad just by looking at them. However, only a few special humans can see the Qilin themselves. It may appear in a kingdom or household that is ruled by wisdom and kindness, or to mark the birth of an exceptionally wise and gentle person.

Despite being so good-natured, a Qilin may become angry if a good person is in danger, and it may breathe flames to chase away anyone cruel or wicked.

BARONG

Much-loved guardian spirit animal from Indonesia

In the mythology of Bali, Indonesia, the Barong is a protective, kind, and brave spirit animal. Different areas can have different Barong animals, but the best-known is the beloved Barong Ket, or Lion Barong. A strange creature, he's a mixture of a lion, a bear, and a giant white dog. His body is covered in long, shaggy white fur, and his head is red, with bulging eyes, sharp tusks, and a long beard.

The king of all spirits, the Barong represents the forces of good. He watches over the people of Bali, and protects their forests and villages. To do this, however, he must fight the forces of evil, in the form of Rangda, the demon queen.

The people of Bali re-enact the battle of Barong and Rangda by performing the Barong dance. Several dancers play the part of the Barong, wearing a white fur costume with a large wooden Barong mask, while another plays Rangda, who appears as a ragged, angry witch. In the dance, Rangda uses evil magic to make Barong's soldiers attack themselves. Barong fights back by using good magic to protect them. At last Barong triumphs, and Rangda runs away. But, according to the legends, no matter how many times Rangda is defeated, she will always return. The battle between good and evil is everlasting, and the Barong must always be ready to fight it.

KURAGE-NO-HINOTAMA

Glowing, fiery jellyfish that float in mid-air

The Kurage-no-Hinotama, or fire jellyfish, is a curious creature of Japanese folklore. A huge jellyfish made of glowing flames, it floats in the air, stinging anyone who gets too close. People are even said to fall prey to a mysterious illness, or even disappear altogether, after encountering one of these eerie jellyfish of the air.

Kurage-no-Hinotama are said to appear close to the sea, but may also haunt marshes and swamps, and even damp underground caverns. According to legend, one moonlit night long ago, a samurai was guarding a temple in Ishikawa, when he saw a Kurage-no-Hinotama approaching him. Startled, the samurai grabbed his sword and slashed at the creature as hard as he could. But the sword seemingly had no effect on it at all, simply slicing through it as if through thin air.

However, the jellyfish did not appreciate the attack. It suddenly spat a red, sticky liquid straight into the terrified samurai's face. Strangely, though, the legend does not reveal what happened next, or whether the unfortunate samurai survived!

TANUKI

*Troublesome, shapeshifting
raccoon dog of Japanese folklore*

Japan has many different *Yokai*, or supernatural
creatures, which feature in folk tales and legends.
One of the most famous is the Tanuki.

Tanuki are real animals, also called raccoon dogs.
They are similar to foxes, but with a raccoon-
like face. In Japanese folklore, however, they are
mischievous, troublemaking tricksters, with magical
abilities. Tanuki can change shape into anything, from
humans and other animals to everyday household objects.
They love making a noise, especially by drumming with their
paws on their big, round bellies, and can imitate other animals,
musical instruments, or even trains.

Tanuki use their sneaky skills to play pranks, tricking people
into getting lost or making fools of themselves. But they
only do it for fun, and are not really evil. In fact,
they can be helpful and friendly, especially to those
who treat them well—as the junk seller in the
story of the Tanuki tea kettle discovered…

The TANUKI TEA KETTLE

One evening, a poor traveling junk seller was sitting by his campfire, warming his hands and having a bottle of sake, a drink made from rice, when he saw a Tanuki approaching from the forest. Now, Tanuki love sake, and when the Tanuki spied the junk seller's open bottle, he asked if he could join him for a drink. The junk seller agreed, and invited the Tanuki to sit down by the fire and share the bottle with him.

The Tanuki was great company. He told the junk seller about all the hilarious shapeshifting tricks he had played on people, and the junk seller told the Tanuki all about how poor he was, because he never had enough things to sell.

"I'll help you, my dear new friend!" declared the Tanuki, since the junk seller, despite being poor, had been so generous to him. "I will turn myself into a practical household item that you will almost certainly be able to sell," he explained.

"Thank you, Tanuki, how very kind of you!" the junk seller exclaimed. But then he fell fast asleep beside the fire.

The next morning, the junk seller awoke with some hazy memories of meeting the Tanuki the night before. "What a strange dream!" he thought. Then, as he gathered up his belongings, he found a good-quality, sturdy-looking tea kettle. It was black, shiny, and surprisingly heavy. The junk seller was delighted, because he knew he could sell the kettle for a good price. That very morning he sold it to a passing monk, ending up with a purse heavy with coins. The monk took the tea kettle back to his kitchen. Pleased with his new purchase, he decided to make a cup of tea straight away, so he filled the kettle with water and put it on to boil. As the base of the kettle began to heat up, the monk heard a strange sound coming from the stove. "Oh, oh, ow, ouch, hot, hot, hot!"

To the monk's astonishment, he saw that his new tea kettle was complaining about the hot stove! Confused, he took the kettle off the heat, and put it on the floor to cool down. The kettle then suddenly grew two furry little legs, and a bushy tail.

"Oooh oooh oooh, my bottom!" said the kettle as it hopped about on its two little legs. Suddenly a little head of a Tanuki popped out on the top of the kettle. And before the monk could stop it, the Tanuki tea kettle ran away, out of the kitchen, through the forest, and back to the campfire.

The monk ran after it, angry that he had been tricked. He demanded his money back, leaving the junk seller as poor as ever.

"I'm sorry," said the Tanuki. "That was all my fault. But don't worry, I have a plan." He told the junk seller to go into town and tie a rope across the square. Then the Tanuki, in the shape of a tea kettle with legs, hopped and danced along the tightrope. Soon, a huge crowd had gathered, and they all paid to see the Tanuki tea kettle walking the tightrope. In this way, the Tanuki helped the junk seller to make his fortune, and he was never poor again.

TSUCHIGUMO

Horrifying and deadly giant human-faced spider

If you're scared of spiders, beware the Tsuchigumo. Its name means "earth spider" in Japanese, and it's a giant, human-sized spider with eight long legs and a hairy, striped body like a tiger's.

Some say Tsuchigumo are normal spiders that have grown very old and reached an enormous size. They live in remote mountains and forests, where they hide in silk-lined burrows. They catch their prey—preferably humans—with long strands of spider silk.

Tsuchigumo can shapeshift into human form, to trick their victims into coming closer in order to trap and eat them. This happened to the great warrior Yorimitsu, in a 1,000-year-old Japanese legend. Yorimitsu and his followers were in the mountains when they saw a flying skull, which they followed. It led them to a remote farm, where they met a beautiful woman. But Yorimitsu knew better than to trust her, suspecting she was really a Tsuchigumo in disguise. He fought her with his sword, and she ran away, leaving a trail of white blood.

Yorimitsu and his men followed the trail up the mountain to a cave, where the Tsuchigumo lurked in its true spider form. Along with his army, Yorimitsu battled the creature until he finally pierced its abdomen. When he did, the skulls of 1,990 of its previous human victims rolled out!

KAWAUSO

Enchanted river-otter tricksters
with shape-changing powers

Kawauso live in the rivers and streams of Japan
and will trick, taunt, and torment anyone
who comes near enough.

Like many cheeky mythical creatures, the Kawauso
can shapeshift and turn into beautiful women, in order
to trick unsuspecting bachelors and make fools of them.
Another favorite game of the Kawauso is to take the form
of an old monk, standing by the river. As you look at him,
the monk grows bigger and bigger, until he's a towering,
terrifying giant. Kawauso also love to give fishermen a fright
by transforming themselves into human heads and getting
themselves caught in fishing nets—before vanishing once
the fisherman has jumped out of his skin in shock.

Kawauso are fond of mimicking sounds, too. As you walk past,
they'll call out your name in a human voice, simply to cause confusion.
When people pass by at night, the Kawauso like to magically
snuff out their lanterns, leaving them lost in the dark.

Sometimes, the Kawauso disguise themselves as humans,
wearing straw hats and clothing, in order to visit shops
to try to buy things. But when anyone speaks
to them, they reply with a stream of nonsense
words, and run away laughing.

KUMIHO

Deadly, liver-devouring, nine-tailed fox of Korea

The Kumiho, or nine-tailed fox, is a Korean legend.
It's also found in Japanese and Chinese folklore, but the
Korean Kumiho is the most gruesome and bloodthirsty.

A Kumiho is created when a fox lives for a thousand
years, grows eight extra tails, and gains shapeshifting
powers. It disguises itself as a young woman to attract
men, who end up dead when the Kumiho eats their
liver, its favorite food. Some say that if a Kumiho completes
a set of tasks, including eating 1,000 livers, it can become
permanently human, and no longer evil.

Even in disguise, telltale signs give the Kumiho away. It may
have strangely pointed ears, or keep its nine tails, covering
them with a long skirt. Its true identity will always appear
in the light of a full moon, however—which is exactly what
happens in the strange tale of the fox sister…

THE TALE OF THE FOX SISTER

A farmer and his wife had three sons, but they longed for a daughter. The farmer wanted a daughter so much that he wished for one, even if she was a fox—a dangerous wish to make. Happily, his wife gave birth to a little girl eventually, to everyone's delight.

The family lived contentedly until the girl was eight years old. One morning, one of the farmer's precious cows was found dead, its body torn open. The farmer had few cows, and could not afford to lose any of them, so he sent his oldest son to watch over the cows at night.

That night, as the brother sat up watching, he saw his little sister sneak out of the farmhouse and approach the cows. To his horror, she tore out a cow's liver. She devoured it ravenously, and the cow fell to the ground, dead. The next morning the boy told his father what had happened.

"What nonsense!" said the farmer, looking at his sweet little daughter playing with her toys. "That's impossible. You must have fallen asleep and had a nightmare." When his son protested that it really had happened, the farmer threw him out of the house.

Still seeking an answer, the farmer sent his second son to guard the cows overnight. Just like his brother, the boy saw his little sister attack and kill a cow and gobble up its liver. But when the boy reported what he had seen, his father was furious and threw him out, too.

The two brothers went to visit a wise old monk for advice.
When they told him what had happened, the monk gave them
three bottles: one white, one red, and one blue. "Take these,"
said the monk, "and use them if danger strikes."

By the light of a full moon, the brothers returned to the farm,
carrying the three bottles. They found the youngest brother
watching over the cows, just as they had done, and sat down next to
him. Just then, their little sister emerged from the farmhouse, heading
toward the cows. As the moonlight shone on her, the brothers suddenly
saw nine tails sticking out from under her long nightdress.

"A fox sister!" gasped one of the brothers. "A Kumiho!" said
another in horror.

The fox sister turned around suddenly, staring at the brothers with
a look of pure evil in her eyes. She lunged toward them, and they realized
that this was no longer the little sister they had once known and loved.

The eldest brother threw down the white bottle, and a thick thorn
hedge sprang from the ground, blocking the girl's path. In a flash
she changed into a nine-tailed fox, and scampered through the thicket.

Next, he threw down the blue bottle. Instantly, a deep river flowed
between the brothers and their fox sister. But she jumped in and
swam across, her fur sleek in the moonlight.

The terrified brothers tried to run away, but the eldest
stumbled and tripped, dropping the red bottle. A wall
of roaring flames rose from the ground between them
and the Kumiho. Unable to stop, it ran straight
into the fire. It burned up and became a tiny
mosquito, which flew away, smoldering, into
the dark forest.

OCEANIA

Oceania stretches across Australia, New Zealand, and the far-flung islands of the South Pacific. Australia's Aboriginal peoples tell stories about the creatures of the Dreaming, the ancient time before humans were created.

TIDDALIK

The thirsty frog of Dreamtime mythology

Tiddalik the frog is one of many creatures found
in the ancient stories of Australia's Aboriginal
peoples. These tales form an important part of
the Aboriginal peoples' beliefs, known as the
Dreaming, which explain how the world was formed
long ago, and why things are the way they are.

The story of Tiddalik was first told by the people of South Gippsland,
in southeastern Australia—but it's become so popular that it
has spread all over the country and around the world. A frog that
can swallow vast amounts of water, Tiddalik may have
originally been based on a real frog species, the water-
holding frog, which stores water in its body to survive
the dry season hiding underground. It's when
Tiddalik wakes up that trouble starts…

TIDDALIK
AND THE FLOOD

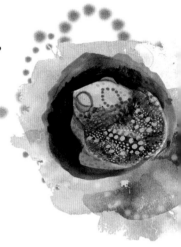

Long, long ago, there lived a frog called Tiddalik. He had buried himself in an underground burrow during a drought, and had fallen asleep for many years. At last, a huge storm broke. Rain hammered on the ground and the sky rumbled with thunder, and Tiddalik finally woke up.

He dug himself out of his hole and looked around. Blinking and yawning, he saw his old friend the platypus. "Platypus!" he said. "It's me, Tiddalik!"

"Tiddalik, where on earth have you been?" said the platypus. "Look how thin you are! You must be so thirsty! Come to the lake and have a drink of water."

Tiddalik was indeed desperate for water. He followed Platypus to the lake and took a few sips. Then he began to take massive, slurping gulps. He was so thirsty, he just couldn't stop.

The other animals watched in amazement as Tiddalik's body began to swell. "Stop!" cried the platypus. "Leave some water for us!" But Tiddalik would not stop. Soon the lake was almost empty, with fish flapping around helplessly in the mud.

"I need MORE water," Tiddalik demanded. He set off for the nearest river and continued to drink all the water he could find. He emptied every lake, pond, and waterhole, until there was no water left anywhere.

The other animals were very worried, because they knew they couldn't live without water. So Wise Owl called a meeting. "I have an idea to get our water back," she said. "If we can make Tiddalik laugh, he might spit out the water." The other animals agreed to try it.

Meanwhile, Tiddalik was finally full, and ready for a nap. He was about to bury himself underground again when the platypus spotted him. "Oh, there you are, Tiddalik!" the platypus called. "Don't go away—we're putting on a show for you, to welcome your return." Tiddalik was flattered by this idea, so he agreed to watch the show.

Each animal came out and tried to make the swollen frog laugh. The kookaburras sang silly songs. The echidna stuck her long tongue out and made faces. The koalas told jokes. Even the lazy crocodile stood up and walked on his hind legs. But Tiddalik was full and tired, and he didn't feel like laughing.

The animals were beginning to panic when Nabunum the eel slithered from behind a rock. At first he twisted and wriggled. Tiddalik didn't find this funny at all. Then the eel tied himself in several knots. Still Tiddalik didn't laugh.

Poor Nabunum gave up, and turned to leave. But he had tied himself in so many knots that he fell over, flat on his face. Tiddalik smiled. Again Nabunum tried to get up and leave, but he fell over once more. Tiddalik giggled, and a little water escaped from his mouth.

Nabunum slithered around on the ground, wriggling so frantically that he tangled himself into one big knot. Suddenly, Tiddalik could not contain his laughter any longer. He gave a huge belly laugh, and all the water came gushing out, flooding the world and filling up all the empty lakes, waterholes, and rivers.

And from that day on, Tiddalik agreed to share the water, and never take more than he needed.

RAINBOW SERPENT

Giant water serpent who brought the world to life

In Aboriginal mythology, the Rainbow Serpent, or Goorialla,
is the source of all life on Earth. The story goes that in the beginning
the world was flat and empty, and all life was asleep. Then, one day,
the Rainbow Serpent woke up and came out of her burrow,
onto the surface. She slithered across the land, carving out
the deep river valleys and pushing up the mountains.

She called to the frogs, who were also hiding underground, their
bellies filled with water. When the frogs came out, the Rainbow
Serpent tickled them, making them spit out all the water,
which flowed into the river valleys and watered the land,
making plants and trees grow. This woke up all the other
animals, and they came out too, and began running,
crawling, swimming, and flying around.

After all this effort, the Rainbow Serpent was tired, so
she slithered into a deep waterhole to relax. To this day,
waterholes are where the beautiful, many-colored serpent
can be found. The animals are always careful not to disturb
her as they drink, so she can continue to rest.

But after a rainstorm, when the rain and wind
churn up the water, the Rainbow Serpent
will rise up and travel across the sky, to find
another waterhole to sleep in. As she goes, she
brightens the world with her colorful stripes,
appearing to humans as a rainbow.

ABAIA

Fierce lake-dwelling Melanesian monster eel

The Abaia comes from the mythology of Melanesia, a scattering of islands in the southwestern Pacific Ocean, including the Solomon Islands, Vanuatu, and Fiji. An Abaia is a giant eel that lives at the bottom of a lake, guarding all the fish and other animals that live there. Many lakes in this region are said to have their own Abaia.

As long as an Abaia's lake is undisturbed, there is no problem. But if anyone tries to catch the fish there, or harms the lake's wildlife in any way, the Abaia gets angry. It sees the animals in its lake as its own children, and will always do whatever it can to protect them. So, with a flick of its enormous tail, it will send waves, rain, or storms to swamp fishing boats or wash away intruders, as some greedy villagers were unlucky enough to discover…

The ABAIA and the old WOMAN

On the island of Fiji, there was a large, beautiful lake, and at the bottom of it lived an Abaia: a giant guardian eel. She had lived there peacefully for a long time, because none of the local villagers had ever discovered the lake. It was hidden between two mountains, with thick undergrowth making it almost impossible for anyone to find a path to its shores.

The creatures in the lake, the Abaia's beloved children, lived in freedom, knowing that nothing would harm them. Unlike many other, less secret lakes, it was a safe, idyllic place. The animals multiplied quickly, with no predators to catch and eat them, until the lake was teeming with many species of fish of all shapes and sizes.

One day, however, a man finally found his way through the thick jungle to the shore of the lake. He could not believe how many fish there were swimming around in the water, and how easy it was to catch them. He loaded up his baskets and carried as many fish as he could back to his village. He had no idea that the lake was home to an Abaia.

That night, the man boasted to his fellow villagers about how many fish he had caught, and what an amazing lake he had found. So the next day the entire village returned with him to see the lake for themselves.

They cast their nets into the beautifully clear water, and, just as the man had described, they caught more fish than they could ever have thought possible—and far more than they needed.

One woman even managed to snag the Abaia with a fishing hook that she threw deep into the middle of the lake. The hook sank down and down and caught the Abaia by her mouth, but she managed to pull free. You can imagine how angry that made the Abaia. She was furious, and resolved to punish the people who had dared to harm her lake and catch the fish that lived there.

The Abaia's enormous tail began to twitch, and she stirred and raised herself from the bottom of the lake. Swirling and circling in the water, she summoned up a mighty rainstorm that flooded the village and flattened the people's crops. Then she thrashed her tail on the surface of the water, creating a giant wave that surged down the mountainside and engulfed the village.

All the people were swept away, except for one. There was a woman living in the village who was very, very old, and very, very wise. She knew about the ways of the Abaia, and had not eaten any of the fish that the villagers had caught. Because of this, the giant eel decided to save her life. As the wave crashed over the village, it carried the old woman along until she came to a tall tree. She grabbed hold of it, then climbed to the top and waited until the water had passed by. And from that day on, she never told another soul about the secret lake, so that the Abaia and her children would be left in peace.

For Bia, Tove & Ernie

With thanks to

Laurence King
Katherine Pitt
Leah Willey
Davina Cheung
Florian Michelet